THE SECRET TO BEING HAPPY

Anahita Hughes

AuthorHouse™ UK
1663 Liberty Drive
Bloomington, IN 47403 USA
www.authorhouse.co.uk
Phone: 0800 047 8203 (Domestic TFN)
+44 1908 723714 (International)

ISBN: 978-1-7283-9580-7 (sc)
ISBN: 978-1-7283-9579-1 (e)

Print information available on the last page.

Published by AuthorHouse 11/19/2019

authorHOUSE

The Secret to Being Happy

Anahita Hughes

In a mystical land far, far away, there once lived a family of dinosaurs. The island that they lived on was made out of body parts, so it was called Body Island. At the top of the island was a gigantic volcano, but it was not just any ordinary volcano. It was Bum Volcano. And surrounding that volcano were massive, white, toilet rolls, which were put there to try and protect the villagers in case of an eruption!

Towards the south part of the island was a cave in the shape of a nose. This was Snot Cave because there was a lagoon of green, slimy, and smelly snot right beneath it that bubbled and oozed pop! Next to the cave was Bone Graveyard, which was full of broken bones and earbuds. It was also the home of the Ungabelly tribe.

On the other side of the island lived a tribe called Ears, who all lived in a big beehive and worshipped Queen Ear. But you couldn't get to her or the ear hive without crossing the dangerous sticky swamp made entirely from earwax.

The dinosaurs lived in the west part of the island near Skully Hill. It was a nice, quiet place with a giant, white, crumbly skull at the top of the grassy green hill. Grey bones were scattered all over the ground. They led to a path to where the dinosaurs lived, which was also far away from Bum Volcano—just in case it erupted. Rumble. Oh no! False alarm!

Mummy Nanda and her two children, Nayanasouraus and Bali, had only recently moved to the island. They hadn't had a chance to explore it yet, but other dinosaurs warned them not to get in the way of or speak to the Ungabelly tribe, who lived at the bottom of the hill as they were at war with the Ears. They came across as very strange because they wore outfits made out of leaves and carried around unused earbuds.

Nayanasouraus, the oldest of the two, was a pinky and bubbly dinosaur. Nayanasouraus, who liked to be called Nayana, loved wearing all kinds of bows and colourful outfits. She enjoyed dancing and acting; she could be very loud and dramatic at times. Her favourite food was chocolate ice cream—as long as it had unicorn sprinkles on top!

Bali was a red, small, and shy dinosaur, the complete opposite of his sister. He liked to be by himself, painting or drawing. He didn't eat meat as he really loved animals and looking after them. He even had a pet called Harry, who was a very furry little creature. Nanda's son's favourite food was sweet potato chips, and he loved ice cream, just like his sister.

As the dinosaurs had recently moved to Body Island, the children had to go to a new school. The next day was Nayana and Bali's first day at Raptor Academy, which was right near Snot cave, where the Ungabelly tribe lived.

They were very excited to meet their new teacher as well as all their classmates. They had joined at just the right time. The school was going on a trip to visit Bum Volcano the next day as they were studying volcanoes! Before they knew it, it was time for break. 'Oh, my goodness. Look at the time! Children, it's break time. Please put away your pencils and books and head out to break,' their teacher said whilst putting their snack box on the table. All the children grabbed their snacks and rushed out to the playground.

In the playground, there were many groups of children. Some played on the swings near the big flowery field. Others were dancing and doing the floss on the gravel. The other children played with the break-time equipment and games near the multicoloured fun shack.

Nayana was standing by herself until she saw a group of girls walk past. They were in her class, so she bravely decided to go up to them and try to make friends. 'Hi, my name is Nayanasouraus, but my friends call me Nayana. What's all of your names?' All the other dinosaurs just looked at her and laughed.

'Why do you have that bow on your head? It looks weird,' said one of the girls. She laughed, and the rest joined in.

'Yeah bows aren't retch anymore,' added another.

'Rada, stop trying to make "retch" happen,' the dinosaur named Kim said. Kim glared evilly at Nayana whilst walking up to her. 'Flowers are in, not bows,' Kim said rudely. She turned to walk away, and all the other girls followed, like little ducklings swimming after their mother.

All of a sudden, the bell went ding, ding, ding! 'Children, please line up and head back to your classes. Um, excuse me.' The teacher glared, hands on her hips, at a group of children in the distance 'The bell has gone, and I have been standing here for over a few minutes now, so why are you children still flossing?' she called firmly as she angrily sped towards that group of children. Nayana, her head hung low, sadly joined the end of the line, and they went back in for their next lesson. As they walked past the children on time out, the ones who continued to floss after the bell rang, Nayana gloomily pulled the bow from her head and threw it on the floor. And as she did, the wind gracefully blew the bow into a big puddle of rainwater.

After their maths class, the children washed their hands and got ready for lunchtime. 'Now children, please put away your maths books. And please put your lids back on the glue sticks,' Said the teacher, looking very stressed. 'Then once you have done that, line up at the door if you are having school dinners.

If you are having anything else, please stay on the carpet.' Most of the children started packing away and tidying their tables, but some by the sink were being silly, blowing bubbles and making a mess. 'Children! Do I need to remind you of our class rule again? Why are we being silly whilst washing our hands?' The teacher was red in the face.

'Miss, Miss,' called one of the little dinosaurs at their table very impatiently.

'Yes, Fleischer, what is it?'

'I can't find my glue stick lid!'

'Argh,' cried the teacher as she abruptly grabbed her coffee mug. 'That's it. Everyone out to lunch. Now!'

All the children rushed to the door to line up. Except for Bali, who sat on the carpet, holding his packed lunchbox. After the teaching assistant, Mrs Lee, did the headcount, Bali joined the end of the line. 'What have you got in your packed lunchbox, Bali? Fish? Lamb? Chicken?' a little dinosaur called Brin asked curiously.

'I have a cheese salad wrap with some grapes.'

'Eww. Did your mum forget to pack your meat?' he asked.

'No. I don't like eating meat,' Bali replied proudly.

'Why? That's really strange, I've never met a dinosaur who doesn't eat meat before.'

The boy left quickly to get his dinner, before Bali could explain or say anything. He went to sit with all the other children, leaving Bali all alone at the end of the white and food-stained dinner table.

When the children arrived home, Mummy Nanda, who had just hung out the smelly washing again for the fiftieth time because of Bum Volcano's farts, asked them how their day was at school. They both looked up at her, shrugged, and then both quickly went up to their rooms. Nanda thought they might just be tired, so she started to make their dinner.

Bali went up to his small room to play with Harry and feed him his dinner. 'Hi, Harry. I didn't have a good day at school. This boy was quite mean to me because he didn't understand or like the fact I don't eat meat. I don't know why, but it made me feel really sad, and it's like I don't want to tell anyone what I believe in anymore.' Bali wiped a tear from his cheek. 'Anyway, how was your day? I really missed you. I wish you could come to school with me.'

Bali pretended that Harry replied. Then he happily carried on stroking and feeding him.

Meanwhile, in Nayana's pink, sparkly, and spotty room, she pulled all of her clothes and bows out of her cupboard and threw them on the floor. 'Stupid bows! I never liked them anyway,' she cried whilst throwing them all out with a dramatic *whoosh!* 'I don't think I have anything with flowers on it,' she wailed.

Mummy Nanda, downstairs making dinner, heard all the banging and crying from upstairs and decided to investigate. 'Children, what's all that noise?' She swiftly put down the knife from chopping the carrots and wiped her hands on her yellow apron.

When Nanda entered her daughter's bedroom, Nayana was lying on a huge pile of clothes and bows. 'Nayana, do you want to tell me why your clothes are all on the floor, and why you are lying on top of them?'

'I can never go back to school. Ever,' Nayanasouraus replied theatrically. 'They are not retch! But flowers are!'

Nanda walked over and helped her up. Then she sat beside her on her flowery bed. 'What are you talking about, and what do you mean you can't go back? You and your brother have a school trip tomorrow. School can't be that bad, can it? Was someone mean to you?'

Nayanasouraus thought about telling her mum what happened at school, but she didn't want her mum to go to the school and make matters worse or for the girls not to like her anymore. So she decided to lie. 'No. I guess I'm just tired, Mum.'

'Well, if you clean up this mountain of mess and come down for dinner, I'll give you some chocolate chip ice cream for dessert?'

'With unicorn sprinkles on top?' asked Nayanasouraus. Her eyes lit up just thinking about it.

'Yes, okay, my little nugget. Deal.'

Nanda then went into Bali's room to check on him quickly. 'How was school, little one?'

Bali was still holding Harry, stroking him gently. 'Hmm, not so good, Mum.'

Nanda sat beside him. 'Do you want to tell me what happened?'

Bali looked up at his mum and replied, 'Maybe I should start eating meat.' Harry screamed, 'Ahh,' jumped out of Bali's hands, and dived into his cage. Crash!

'Why, Bali? Why the change of heart all of a sudden?'

'Well, everyone else at my school eats meat. I'm the only one in my class who doesn't.' Sadly, Bali put his head down on Nanda's lap.

'Bali, just because everyone does something doesn't make it right. And just because you believe or do something differently than others doesn't mean you can't still be friends with them. Unless they are unkind or don't respect what you do or believe in, and then in that case, they are not worthy of being your friend.'

Bali smiled and gave his mum a great big hug. Harry also smiled and wiped his forehead with relief. Phew!

The next day, the children all arrived at school early as they were off on their school trip to visit Bum Volcano. Bali had his packed lunch. Nayanasouraus also had hers, as well as a flower from her mum's vase instead of a bow on her head. The children were all very excited. So were the teachers, even though they had to do over a million risk assessments for this trip! 'Now children,' one of the teachers began, 'I hope you have all remembered your packed lunches and remembered to bring them in a paper bag and not—'

'A plastic one! Just say no to plastic to save our planet,' shouted one of the children from the back.

'Yes, well done, Lali! You can have ten raptor points! Remember to all stay together and with your partner when we get off the school bus. And Rocky, no stop that. Boys!' Mrs Stone began to tell off the boys at the back who started to make fart noises with their armpits.

When they arrived, Mrs Stone did a headcount as they got off the big yellow school bus. 'Brilliant, we are all here. Now children, I need to remind you we need to be very careful as this is a real, live volcano. Even though it hasn't erupted for over a hundred years, well, you never know. So if we need to make an emergency exit, following the risk assessment, we sensibly run back to the school bus, leaving packed lunches behind.' The children then paired up and followed Mrs Stone, who continued to ramble on about the history of Bum Volcano.

Bali and his sister were in different groups. He was paired with Brin, the boy who commented on his lunch yesterday. He asked Bali, 'What are you eating today? A few peas and some carrots?' Brin chuckled.

Bali tried to stand up for himself and said as he reached in his packed lunch bag, 'Actually no. I have a ...' Bali paused as he felt something hairy, moving, and rustling in the bag. 'Harry! What are you doing in my lunch bag?'

'Oh, wow! Live lunch. Nice! Can I have some?' Brin evilly licked his lips and slurped as he went to grab Harry.

'No! He's my pet,' Bali cried protectively as he pulled Harry close to him.

HE

NOO

'That's not a pet. That's my lunch!' Quick as flash, Brin grabbed Harry and opened his mouth wide, ready to munch on him with his sharp, shiny, pearly teeth!

'Help me!' squealed a tiny voice. Bali shook, biting his nails, helplessly watching Harry being dangled over the sharp cave of teeth.

'Please don't eat him. He's my friend!' But Brin did not care and lowered Harry on to his wet, slimy, red tongue. 'Nooo!' Suddenly, Bali dived towards him, grabbing Harry as quick as a thief stealing money from a bank. And without thinking, he started to run up the side of the volcano!

As Bali was about to reach the top, he could hear Mrs Stone shout frantically for him to come down. But he was just too upset and worried for Harry to even stop. Finally, Bali stopped when he reached the top and nearly fell inside Bum Volcano! 'Don't worry, Harry, I won't let him hurt you!'

GET DOWN BALI !!!

Suddenly, Bali felt the ground start to shake. 'Oh, no! Children, back to the school bus!' Mrs Stone frantically tried to round up all the children, but Bali was still at the top of the volcano.

'It's gonna blow,' cried one of the children.

'Bali, get down!' Nayana yelled to her brother.

Bali couldn't hear his sister, so she decided to run to the top and get him. As she struggled up the side of the volcano, Bali headed back down towards her. 'What are doing?' she yelled at him.

'That mean boy was going to eat Harry and said I was weird for not eating meat, and ...' The ground was still shaking.

'Bali, we haven't got time for this. The volcano is going to—'

Suddenly, Bum Volcano let out the loudest fart in the world! *Bang!* A huge amount of brown smoke wafted down the hill. The stench was so strong, it made poor Nayana and Bali faint and fall to the ground. *Thud.*

'Heeya, heeya, heyya. Heyya, heyya, heyya.' A weird humming sound woke up Bali and Nayanasouraus.

'Where are we? Are we dead?' Bali looked around curiously, rubbing his eyes.

'We are in a cave, silly,' answered Nayana. 'How did we get here, though? And what's that sound? It sounds like a big bee.'

'I don't know, but it's coming from that direction,' Bali said, pointing towards the mouth of the cave.

They helped each other up and walked towards the mysterious sound. As they stepped outside the dark, gloomy cave, they realised that they were in Bone Graveyard, home to the Ungabelly tribe.

'We are in Bone Graveyard, Nayana! Mum warned us that we shouldn't go here or talk to the Ungabelly tribe. She heard they were weird!'

'How did we get here, though, Bali?' Nayana asked with a very confused look on her face.

'Greetings, dinos. My name is Devi. I am king of the Ungabelly tribe. We saved you from Bum Volcano's stench.' A hairy man wearing a leaf skirt and holding an earbud graciously appeared before them.

'You saved us?' Nayana asked, trying to not look so surprised.

'Yes, You both were knocked out on the floor from the stench. We could not just leave you there. We look after everyone and everything in my village and on this island,' the king said proudly.

'Oh, thank you so much. I feel really badly now. We heard you all weren't very nice, but I guess that was wrong.'

'Well, you should never believe rumours or judge a book by its cover. You were both very lucky that the Ears did not find you first. Otherwise, you would be covered in earwax right now, captured and left in their swamp.'

'Oh, thank you so much, Mr Devi. My name's Bali, by the way. And this is my sister. And this is ...' Bali reached for Harry and realised he wasn't there. 'Oh, no! Harry!'

'Harry? Is this Harry you speak of a small and furry creature?'

'Yes! Yes! Have you seen him?'

The king reached behind him and took something from one of his servants. He presented Bali a very well-groomed Harry, who was now wearing a leaf skirt and holding a mini-earbud too!

'Oh, Harry, you're safe,' Bali said as he hugged him.

'Thank you so much for saving us. But we really should get home. Our mum is probably really concerned about us,' Nayanasouraus said worriedly.

'It is okay. Do not worry. I sent my people up to Skully Hill to fetch your mother, so please, come sit, rest, and wait by the fire.' They gathered around the fire while the servants fanned them with great big leaves.

'I am curious, though. Why were you children up at Bum Volcano?'

Nayanasouraus looked over at her brother, giving him *the* look.

Bali cleared his throat and replied, 'Well, you see, this boy was being mean to me at school because of what I eat and believe in. He then tried to eat Harry. So I needed to get away from him and ran. To be honest, I'm not really enjoying school because I'm very different from the rest of my class.'

'Me too,' Nayanasouraus replied softly. 'Some of the girls at school made fun of what I was wearing. And because of it, I threw away all my bows and tried to wear what they were wearing. But they still didn't want to sit next to me.'

King Devi looked at them whilst tapping his earbud to the ground. 'Children, let me show you something.' The king led the children over to a beautiful forest with lots of trees. But one ginormous tree right in the center stuck out. It was over a hundred feet high and had many flowers on it. 'Many years ago, my great-great-grandfather planted this tree, but for many months, it would not grow. Do you know why this tree would not grow, children?'

'Hmm, maybe because he never watered it,' guessed Bali.

'Or maybe the sun did not get to it,' Nayanasouraus said.

'Incorrect,' King Devi said sharply as he went up and placed his hand softly on the tree. 'My great-great-grandfather watered the tree and made sure it was in sunlight. But he was doing it all wrong because he was watering the leaves.'

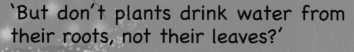

'But don't plants drink water from their roots, not their leaves?'

'Exactly, Nayanasouraus! You cannot change things on the outside and then expect those things to make you happy on the inside because it all starts from within.'

'So did it start to grow after he watered the roots?' Bali asked, looking up at the enormous tree.

'Yes. But the reason it grew to be the tallest and the most beautiful tree of all was because he also loved the tree very much.'

At that moment, Nanda came racing in. 'Children! Oh, my goodness! I was so worried about you both. I went up to the school to pick you up, and they said you ran up the side of the Bum Volcano and that they had to leave you there! I nearly fainted, but these Ungabelly people came and told me they rescued you both! Oh, children, are you okay?' She was nearly crying whilst hugging them so tightly that they almost couldn't breathe. 'Mr Ungabelly tribe man, thank you so, so much.'

'Mum, he's the king! And his name is Devi,' Bali said, struggling for air.

'Oh, my goodness, my apologies, my lord.' Nanda turned towards him and tried to bow to the king whilst kissing his hand.

Nayanasouraus and Bali rolled over, giggling in the background, watching their mum.

The dinosaurs thanked all of the Ungabelly tribe and headed home. On their way back, they told their mum all about what had happened at school and why they ended up at the top of Bum Volcano.

'Oh, children, I wish you had spoken to me sooner.'

'Well, Mr Devi showed us this tree that was the biggest in the forest, and it only got big, Mum, because he watered it from the roots. Plus, he loved it! I want to be as big as that tree, Mum,' Bali said, smiling.

'What great advice that Mr Devi gave. And you can be whatever you want.' Nanda stopped and knelt in front of her children. 'Little ones, I'm going to tell you a big secret. Are you ready?' The children nodded in excited anticipation.

'The secret to being happy is to love yourself first.'

'Isn't that being selfish, Mum?' Nayana asked.

'No, self-love is not selfish, nugget, because you cannot truly love or look after someone unless you love yourself first. For example, if I wanted to pour some of my drink into your cup because you were thirsty but I had an empty cup, how would I give you a drink?'

'You couldn't! You need to make yourself one first, Mum!' Bali said.

'Exactly, my little one. And because I am proud of who I am and love myself, I have lots more love for the both of you. And Mr Devi is right. You need to water your roots, not your leaves.'

'But I don't have any leaves, Mum.' Bali looked confused.

Nayana and Nanda looked at each other and laughed. 'What Mum is trying to say, Bali, is that we shouldn't feel we need to change for other people. I shouldn't want to change my bows and wear flowers just to try and fit in with those girls at school. That will never truly make me happy. And Bali, we need to be happy with who we are and what we do, no matter what other people say.' Nayana threw the flower out of her hair and into the air. She hugged her brother tightly.

Nanda asked Bali if he then understood. 'Yes, Mummy, I do! I have to be proud of myself too. I won't let anyone upset me over what I eat or believe in because I'm watering my roots and love myself,' Bali shouted as he jumped up into the air.

The three of them hugged and smiled.

From that day on, the children knew that the secret to happiness was to love themselves, no matter what anyone else thought. And they all lived happily after.

Are you watering your roots?

Can you make a list of all of the things you love about yourself?

Lightning Source UK Ltd.
Milton Keynes UK
UKHW051530121219
355223UK00003B/81/P